DOCTOR·WHO

THE CYBERMEN

BBC CHILDREN'S BOOKS
Published by the Penguin Group
Penguin Books Ltd, 80 Strand, London, WC2R 0RL, England
Penguin Group (USA), Inc., 375 Hudson Street, New York, New York 10014, USA
Penguin Books (Australia) Ltd, 250 Camberwell Road, Camberwell, Victoria 3124, Australia.
(A division of Pearson Australia Group Pty Ltd)
Canada, India, New Zealand, South Africa.
Published by BBC Children's Books, 2006
Text and design © Children's Character Books, 2006
Images © BBC 2004
Written by Justin Richards
10 9 8 7
Printed in China.
ISBN-13: 978-1-40590-249-6

CONTENTS

The Cybermen

Meet the Cybermen 4
Cyber Data 6
Cyber Anatomy 8
◆ Test your Knowledge

Cyber Allies

John Lumic 10
The Cyber Controller 11
Controlled Humans 12
The Army of Ghosts 13
◆ Test your Knowledge

Cyber Enemies

The Doctor 14
The Preachers 15
Pete Tyler 16
The Daleks 17
◆ Test your Knowledge

Cyber Origins

The 'Other' Earth 18
The Arrival of the Cybermen 20
◆ Test your Knowledge

Weapons and Technology

Cybus Industries 22
Built-in Accessories 24
◆ Test your Knowledge

Cyber Encounters 26
◆ Test your Knowledge

Test your Knowledge Answers 30

Going off the Rails 31

They might look like tall, deadly, metal robots, but the Cybermen are more terrifying than that. They used to be like us. But their limbs and bodily organs were replaced with artificial ones. Plastic and steel replaced flesh and blood; motors and electronics replaced muscles and nerves. Even the brains were changed. An emotional inhibitor made sure that the Cybermen would no longer feel pain or anger, or fear or love...

The result was a more efficient, more hard-wearing sort of person. They were stronger; they didn't tire or need to sleep. They could survive without air or food or water... But they were no longer human. They might not have emotions, but they did have one ambition: to survive at all costs.

And so they converted more and more people into Cybermen, into bloodless, fleshless, soulless robots that used to be people. And deep inside, hidden away as if they are ashamed of it, there is still some flesh, some bone, some brain, some bits of humanity preserved amongst the plastic and metal. And perhaps, deep inside, there is also a memory of who they once were, and just possibly regret...

Name: Cybermen

Species: Adapted Human

Height: Over 2m (over 6'7")

Home planet: A parallel Earth

Weaponry: Inbuilt energy blaster

Protection: Metal armour

Invented by: John Lumic

Manufactured by: Cybus Industries

Construction: Plastic and steel

Leader: The Cyber Controller

CYBER ANATOMY

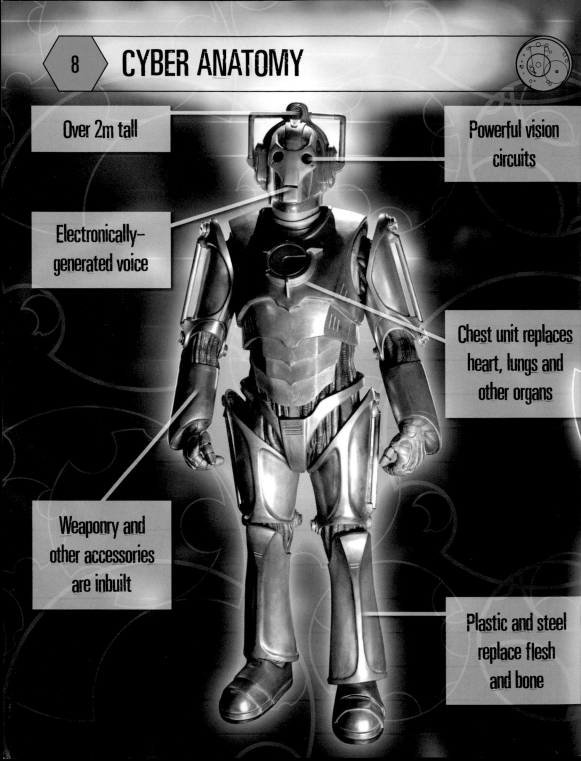

Over 2m tall

Powerful vision circuits

Electronically-generated voice

Chest unit replaces heart, lungs and other organs

Weaponry and other accessories are inbuilt

Plastic and steel replace flesh and bone

TEST YOUR
KNOWLEDGE

JOHN LUMIC

On another Earth, very like our own planet but in another universe running parallel to ours, a man called John Lumic invented the Cybermen. He saw Cybermen as an extension of our own evolution — an upgrade to humanity like computers and software programs get upgraded. He thought that turning people into Cybermen would be an *improvement*.

He was already very ill and in a special wheelchair, but even so he was unwilling to be upgraded himself until the moment he died. The Cybermen he had created had other ideas and made him into their Cyber Controller.

THE CYBER CONTROLLER

The Controller is the leader of the Cybermen. He used to be John Lumic, the man who created the Cybermen in the first place. The Controller is wired into a special throne and special pipes feed nutrient fluids and power into his body. When the Doctor, Rose and their friends destroyed the Cybermen, the Controller survived. He broke free of his throne and attacked them.

After the Cyber Controller was destroyed, Cybermen who survived were commanded by Cyberleaders. You can recognise a Cyberleader because the rods attached to their helmets are black instead of silver.

CONTROLLED HUMANS

The Cybermen can control humans who are not completely Cybermen using special headsets. These headsets look rather like the earpieces some people wear to use their mobile phones, and they feed Cyber instructions directly into the person's brain. The people taken over by the Cybermen no longer have any will power of their own, and are entirely controlled by the Cybermen.

Be careful when you see someone wearing one of these earpieces. Of course, they might just be using their mobile phone, but they *could* be a Cyberman agent!

THE ARMY OF GHOSTS

When ghostly figures first started to appear, there was panic. People were afraid of the faint, grey figures that appeared around the world. But after a while they decided that the ghosts meant them no harm. They thought that loved ones who had died were now coming back to visit their friends and relatives.

But that was not the case. The ghosts were the first hint that the Cybermen were coming. They had found a way through from another parallel world into our own universe. When at last they appeared fully, people realised their mistake. But by then it was too late — the Cybermen had already invaded. Millions of them were now on earth, ready to turn us all into creatures like them: Cybermen.

TEST YOUR KNOWLEDGE

THE DOCTOR

The Doctor is the last of the Time Lords, a powerful race that had the secret of travel through time and space, but was destroyed in a Great Time War. The Doctor is the greatest enemy of the Cybermen and has defeated them in many times and places throughout his many lives.

The Doctor can change his appearance. When his body is worn out or damaged he can change into a new one. Travelling through space and time in his TARDIS and with the help of various companions, the Doctor fights against evil and injustice. He has met the Cybermen before, in our universe. So it was a big surprise for him to discover that Cybermen were being created on another version of Earth — a parallel world very like our own.

THE PREACHERS

The Preachers are opposed to the way the large corporation Cybus Industries is taking over the world and are determined to stop it. They are led by Ricky — a parallel version of Mickey Smith who lives in the other Earth. Mickey teamed up with the Preachers to help defeat Cybus and fight the Cybermen.

The other Preachers are Jake and Mrs Moore. They travel in a special van kitted out with equipment. The Preachers get their information about Cybus from a spy inside the company — they don't know who it really is, but the man calls himself 'Gemini'.

PETE TYLER

The Doctor's best friend and companion is Rose Tyler. Her dad died when she was a baby, but in the other world where the Cybermen were created, Rose's dad is still alive.

Pete Tyler works for John Lumic at Cybus Industries. But he is secretly sending out information about Lumic's plans, using the code name Gemini. When he finds he is broadcasting the information only to the Preachers he is disappointed. But they all work together — Pete, the Preachers, Rose, Mickey and the Doctor — and defeat the Cybermen.

When the Cybermen escape from Pete's world into our world, he follows to fight their evil wherever it appears.

THE DALEKS

Hated and feared throughout the whole universe, the Daleks are the most ruthless and evil creatures in all creation. They might look like robots, but inside that protective, armoured shell is a living creature. It was thought that they were all destroyed in a Great Time War against the Time Lords — the Doctor's people. But some survived.

The Cult of Skaro was a special group of Daleks that hid in the void between universes to wait for the Time War to end. Then they arrived on Earth, but their Void Ship left a trail that the Cybermen were able to follow to invade our world. While the Daleks and Cybermen fought a tremendous battle, the Doctor was able to defeat them both.

TEST YOUR KNOWLEDGE

CYBER ORIGINS

THE 'OTHER' EARTH

Rose and Mickey thought they were back in London when the TARDIS arrived on the other version of Earth. But soon they knew that the Doctor's TARDIS had brought them to another Earth — like our own world, but also very different. The London skyline was odd and there were large airships, zeppelins, in the sky over the city.

On this world, Rose had never been born, but her father was still alive. And Mickey was called Ricky. It was a strange moment when Mickey and Ricky met.

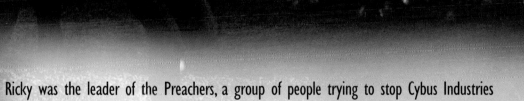

Ricky was the leader of the Preachers, a group of people trying to stop Cybus Industries from getting too powerful.

With communications technology further advanced on this other world than on our own, Cybus Industries was able to control people through special earpieces. People thought they were just getting the latest news, weather and sports information from the earpieces. But in fact Cybus was getting ready to take over. Even the Preachers did not know what Cybus was really doing.

They were taking homeless people off the streets and turning them into the first Cybermen. It was up to the Doctor and his friends, with help from the Preachers, to stop them...

THE ARRIVAL OF THE CYBERMEN

Rose and the Doctor arrived back on Earth, and were introduced to a ghost! Rose's mum, Jackie, thought it was the ghost of her father. All over the world ghosts were appearing and people thought they were the spirits of their dead friends and relatives. At first people were scared and worried, but after a while they got used to the 'ghosts' being around and accepted they meant no harm.

But people were wrong. The faint cloudy shapes were not ghosts. They were the Cybermen breaking through into our world as they escaped from their own parallel Earth.

A secret group of scientists and soldiers called Torchwood was trying to find out more about the ghosts and actually bringing them through. The Cybermen took over some of the people at Torchwood and got them to open the doorway between the universes so they could come through properly.

People saw what was happening when the Cybermen became solid — it was an invasion. Millions of Cybermen arrived all over the world, and no one could stop them. No one except the Doctor and Rose.

TEST YOUR KNOWLEDGE

CYBUS INDUSTRIES

Cybus Industries is one of the largest communications and technology companies in the world. It is so important that even the President has to listen to what they say, though he doesn't always like it. In fact, the President tried to stop the Cybus Industries project to upgrade humanity to the next level. But by the time he tried to act, it was too late and the Cybermen had taken over.

Cybus Industries also owns lots of other companies, such as International Electromatics. Together with these, Cybus provides information like news, weather, television and even winning lottery numbers. It also provides the technology so that people can receive that information. They get it sent directly to special earpieces that let them hear and see the broadcasts. The information is downloaded directly into people's brains.

But Cybus can control the earpieces, and use them to take people over. The affected people walk calmly, unthinking, into vast Cybus factories, where they are adapted and changed into more Cybermen.

BUILT-IN ACCESSORIES

Designed by a technology company, the Cybermen have many accessories and functions that are built directly into them. The Cyberman's weaponry, for example, is part of the forearm. A high-energy blaster emerges from the arm and the Cyberman aims using a heads-up display in the eye circuits. This targeting system is linked directly to the Cyberman's arm to make sure that the gun is always on target.

As well as, or instead of, the standard weaponry, Cybermen may have other facilities built into the forearm. A Cyberman with an arm-mounted camera can broadcast the demands of its Cyberleader across a planet's own communications system by hacking into it.

TEST YOUR KNOWLEDGE

In addition to standard communications between Cybermen, they can also download information from one to another. In the event that a Cyberleader is destroyed, its entire data set and memory can be downloaded into another Cyberman. That Cyberman then becomes the Cyberleader — with all the experience, tactical expertise and knowledge of the original.

The Doctor arrived on Earth with his friends Rose and Mickey. Or so they thought. But London looked very different — with huge zeppelins in the sky. They realised they were not on our world, but *another* Earth which was similar but also very different. They found that a large company called Cybus Industries provided people with information, entertainment and news through special earpieces. But they also found that the owner of Cybus Industries — a man called John Lumic — wanted to 'upgrade' people as if they were computer products. He wanted to turn them into Cybermen.

With the help of a group of people called the Preachers, who were opposed to what Cybus was trying to do, the Doctor and his friends managed to get into the factory where the Cybermen were being made. Mickey used Rose's mobile phone to jam the signal that blocked off the Cybermen's emotions. That meant that all the people who had been turned into Cybermen suddenly remembered who they had been and realised what had happened to them. The shock was so great that the Cybermen all died. All except John Lumic, who had been turned into the Cyber Controller. He tried to stop the Doctor, but he failed.

With the Cybermen defeated in London, Mickey and the Preachers were left to find out if there were more Cybus Industries factories in other cities, waiting to produce Cybermen...

Mickey and the Preachers found that there were other Cybermen, and they were too late to stop them. But the Cybermen decided to escape from their world and found a way to get through the void between universes to reach our own Earth. They appeared only faintly at first — just vague outlines of figures which people thought were ghosts.

However, when scientists at a secret organisation called Torchwood interfered, the Cybermen were able to arrive fully in our world. Millions of Cybermen were invading and no one could stop them.

Then the Doctor and Rose realised it was even worse than that. The Cybermen had followed a strange sphere through the void — a Void Ship. When it opened, everyone expected there would be more Cybermen inside, but there weren't. The ship belonged to the Daleks, and Earth was being invaded not just by Cybermen, but by Daleks as well.

The Daleks and Cybermen fought but, even though there were millions of them, the Cybermen were no match for the Daleks. While the two evil races were battling it out, the Doctor and Rose managed to find a way to get rid of both the Cybermen and the Daleks and Earth was saved.

TEST YOUR KNOWLEDGE

ANSWERS

Meet the Cybermen
1 (b) 2 (c) 3 (a) 4 (b) 5 (c)

Cyber Allies
1 (b) 2 (a) 3 (b) 4 (c) 5 (a)

Cyber Enemies
1 (a) 2 (a) 3 (b) 4 (c) 5 (b)

Cyber Origins
1 (b) 2 (c) 3 (a) 4 (c) 5 (b)

Weapons and Technology
1 (b) 2 (a) 3 (c) 4 (b) 5 (a)

Cyber Encounters
1 (c) 2 (b) 3 (a) 4 (b) 5 (c)

GOING OFF THE RAILS

"It's finished," Sam told Harry during break. Harry knew she'd wanted to tell him something all morning. But Miss Findle had made sure they were on different tables because they talked and mucked about.

Harry knew at once what Sam was talking about. "When can I come and see it?" he asked.

Harry's mum was happy for him to go round to Sam's after school. She stood at the door until she saw Harry go inside Sam's house. Sam's mum said hello to Harry, but he wasn't listening. He and Sam were already running upstairs to the loft.

"Wow!" Harry said as soon as he went into the big room with its sloping walls.

"It's great, isn't it?" Sam said.

"It's brilliant."

Sam's dad had finally finished the train set he'd been building for years. It filled the whole room. There were loads of tracks running through a miniature landscape. There was a town, hills and fields, bridges and hedges. Little cows and sheep stood in the little fields, and tiny cars and lorries were on the narrow roads and lanes.

And through it all the trains ran – old-fashioned steam trains. They played and played until it was dark and Sam's mum had to walk back with Harry and say sorry to his mum for keeping him so long.

"Oh it's all right," Harry's mum said with a laugh. "His dad's not back from the new job yet."

"When's dad going to finish our train set?" Harry asked.

"One day," his mum said. But Harry could tell she

didn't really believe that.

"He's never going to get it finished," Harry complained to Sam next day at school. "We got our set the same day your dad got yours, remember?"

"Why don't we finish it then?" Sam said.

"There's lots to do still," Harry warned her. But it was a brilliant idea.

"We need to start right away then," Sam told him. "I'll come round after school today."

Harry's dad had set up the trains in the garage. It was a much smaller layout than Sam's, and it was hardly even started. Not all the track was laid out and none of it was fixed down on the big board that stood on old packing cases and took up one end of the garage.

"There's not much room to work," Sam complained. "What's all this stuff?"

Alongside the train board was a heap of stuff Harry's dad had brought home when his job finished and he had to move to another factory.

"I think it's just junk," he said. "There was some sort of trouble at the factory. It closed down and the police and the army came." He shrugged. "Anyway, Dad said it was a shame all that work would be wasted and he brought this stuff out."

Sam was looking through the pile of metal and plastic. "Hey look," she said. "I think this is a head. A metal head."

It was stained and dented, but it was certainly a head. It was strange, with blank staring eyes and rods coming out of where the ears should be, that connected to the top of the head. It was big and heavy and when Sam put it down on the edge of the train board, Harry thought the blank face was watching him as he tested a steam train on the loop of track.

The train was hesitant and jerked as it moved. But it ran round the loop, then into a siding. The track just stopped at the end of the siding, and the train came off the end. Sam laughed. "You need to clean the rails, they're dusty," she said.

Then she went back to looking through the pile of junk. Sam liked making things, she always had. Now she was pulling out bits and pieces from the pile and stacking them on the edge of the board.

"I thought we were getting the train set finished,"

Harry said.

"In a minute. Look." Sam held up a metal hand, complete with jointed silver fingers. "I think there's a whole metal man here. Metal and plastic." She held up a long, jointed arm. It looked very heavy and she could only just lift it.

Harry put down the train and helped Sam. In the middle of the pile, they found the metal man's body, with both legs and one arm still attached. Sam pushed the hand on to the end of the wrist, and it clicked into place. "Let's put him back together," she said.

The other pieces clicked back into place easily too. Soon they had a complete figure. Between them they managed to drag the heavy metal man to an old chair, and pushed it into a sitting position. Sam picked up the head and perched it on top of the neck.

"It's huge," Harry said.

"He can watch us do the trains," Sam said. "We'll have to think of a good name for him."

They worked on the train set for a long time. Sam got several of the engines working and soon they were whizzing round the track. Harry found that by turning the dial that sent power to the trains, he could make them go really fast.

Sam was planning where to put hills and a tunnel when the metal man suddenly stood up. With a clanking, whirring sound it pulled itself to its feet. Sam and Harry stared in astonishment, and the metal head turned to look at them.

The metal man's voice was a mechanical rasp. "I

am complete," it said, and its mouth glowed as it spoke. "All systems re-linked and repaired. Two young humans detected." It looked at them through its deep, dark, empty eyes. "They will be upgraded."

"What are you?" Harry said. He was frightened and his voice was trembling as much as the rest of him.

"Did we make you?" Sam asked. She sounded afraid too, but proud at the same time.

"You initiated self-repair systems. I am a Cyberman."

"I don't like it," Harry said quietly to Sam. "How do we turn it off?"

The Cyberman was still watching them. "Like or dislike is unimportant," it said. "I cannot be turned off. I will survive. You will stay here to be upgraded."

"What do you mean, upgraded?" Sam asked nervously. "We're not machines."

The Cyberman's head turned slightly so it was looking straight at her. "You will be."

The Cyberman was between the children and the door of the garage. They would have to get past it to escape.

"My dad will be home soon," Harry said bravely. "He'll come looking for us."

"Then he will also be upgraded," the Cyberman said. There was no feeling or variation in its voice. It was just flat and mechanical, and chilling. "Try to leave, and I will disable you." It turned to examine the other things Harry's dad had brought from the factory. "Do you understand electronics?"

"I do," Sam said. "A bit."

"Not me," Harry confessed. "It will be time for tea soon. We have to go."

The Cyberman pointed at Harry. "You will remain where you are." Then it pointed at Sam. "You will help build the upgrade equipment. Come here."

Sam looked at Harry, but they both knew she had no choice. She had to help the Cyberman.

Harry felt so useless as he watched. The Cyberman was giving Sam things from the pile of stuff – electronics and meters and dials and cables. It was telling Sam which pieces to fit together. Every now and then Sam looked over at Harry, and every time she did she looked more scared.

Eventually Sam and the Cyberman had built a large

piece of strange-looking equipment. The Cyberman connected it to a power socket in the wall, and the whole thing throbbed with power.

"Is it dangerous?" Harry asked. He was fiddling with one of the toy steam engines. It was quite a chunky design and very heavy for its size. He set it down on the track.

"There's a lot of power being generated. Touch the wrong bit and boom!" Sam clapped her hands together and whooshed them out into an explosion. "There are lots of exposed wires."

"It will suffice," the Cyberman said. "Now you will be upgraded."

"What are you going to do?" Sam asked, backing away towards the train board as the Cyberman reached out for her.

"I will electrify your brain and burn out your resistance and emotions. Replacement of your body parts will follow when components are available."

Harry was nervously turning the dial on the control box for the train set. The steam engine started slowly round the track. As he watched it, and tried not to think about what the Cyberman was saying and what was going to happen to him and Sam, Harry had an idea. He reached over and changed the points.

The Cyberman had almost reached Sam. She was shaking her head and Harry could see the tears in her eyes. He could see her frightened face reflected in the chest of the Cyberman. He hoped his plan would work, but the Cyberman was in the wrong place. The train gathered speed as Harry turned the control dial further.

"Are you coming for tea?"

The voice was calling from outside the door. Harry's mum was outside – about to come in. But if she did the Cyberman would surely get her.

At the sound of Harry's mum's voice, the Cyberman paused. It turned slightly. As it did, Harry managed to catch Sam's eye, and he saw that his friend understood what he was doing. "Now!" Harry shouted.

Sam pushed the Cyberman as hard as she could. The Cyberman took a step sideways. It wasn't far, but it was far enough. Harry twisted the control dial as far as it would go.

The Cyberman turned to face Harry, as if guessing

he had a plan. Or perhaps it had heard the train picking up speed. Perhaps it had seen the heavy metal steam engine hurtling along the siding, towards where the track ended.

The train shot off the end of the siding and across the board. The Cybermen turned for Sam again. The handle of the garage door started to turn.

The heavy metal engine flew off the end of the board. It smashed into the Cyberman's chest just as it was reaching to catch Sam. It was off balance, and the impact of the train hitting it was enough to make the Cyberman stagger back...

And into the humming equipment. The Cyberman's hand went right into the middle of the wires and machinery. Sparks spat across it. Blue fire surrounded the Cyberman's arm like lightning. For a moment it stood upright and still as Harry grabbed Sam's hand and they ran for the door.

As they ran past, the Cyberman staggered again, right into the sparking machinery. It seemed to collapse into it. The equipment fell apart and a sheet of flame shot across the garage accompanied by the roar of an explosion. Smoke drifted through the air.

"What are you up to?" Harry's mum asked from the doorway. "I hope you haven't broken anything."

Harry looked at Sam, and she grinned back at him. "I hope we have," he said quietly.

Behind them, the blistered, scorched head of the Cyberman fell from its shattered body and crashed lifelessly to the floor.

DOCTOR · WHO

OTHER GREAT FILES TO COLLECT

1. The Doctor
2. Rose
3. The Slitheen
4. The Sycorax
5. Mickey
6. K-9
7. The Daleks
8. The Cybermen